Marilla, Michaela, Miles

dream, believe, create!
Leighann Irwin

Gary Iqili '22

Gary Intili

To my granddaughter Elliana, thank you for coming into this world, and to my wife Dawn, who refused to let me remove the pond and install a pizza oven in its place.

Leighann Troino

To my daughter Elliana and my husband Anthony, may you always find adventure in the everyday.

www.mascotbooks.com

Brightly Pond: The Adventures of Fribbit the Frog:
Fribbit's First Adventure

For more information, please contact:
Mascot Books, an imprint of Amplify Publishing Group
620 Herndon Parkway, Suite 320
Herndon, VA 20170
info@mascotbooks.com

Library of Congress Control Number: 2022900630

CPSIA Code: PRT0322A

ISBN-13: 978-1-63755-182-0

Printed in the United States

Brightly Pond:
THE Adventures
OF FRIBBIT THE FROG:
FRIBBIT'S FIRST ADVENTURE

Gary Intili and
Leighann Troino
Illustrated by Alejandro Echavez

Fribbit Frog's big day had finally arrived.

Young Fribbit Frog was excited because today would be his first adventure. His mother, Ribbit Frog, had agreed to let him walk all by himself from their home at Brightly Pond to the other end of Timber Mill Farm to see his friends. He had waited a long time to travel on his own to see Polly Pig and Billy Bull.

"This is going to be fun!" Fribbit Frog cheered.

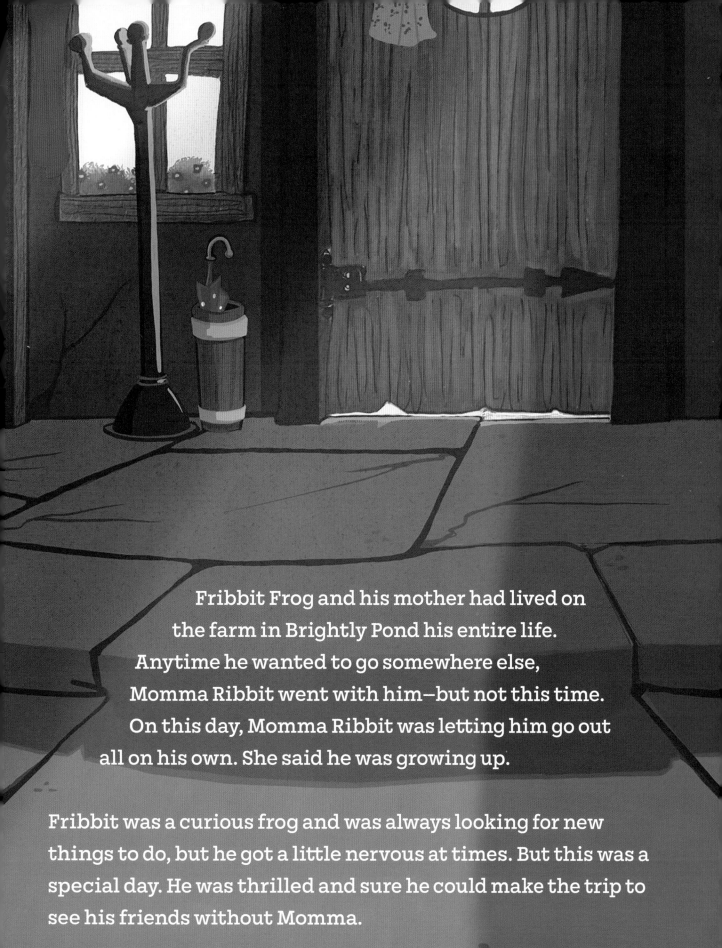

Fribbit Frog and his mother had lived on
the farm in Brightly Pond his entire life.
Anytime he wanted to go somewhere else,
Momma Ribbit went with him—but not this time.
On this day, Momma Ribbit was letting him go out
all on his own. She said he was growing up.

Fribbit was a curious frog and was always looking for new
things to do, but he got a little nervous at times. But this was a
special day. He was thrilled and sure he could make the trip to
see his friends without Momma.

After finishing his
morning chores and having
lunch, Fribbit was ready to head out
to see his friends. He couldn't wait to
tell everyone at the pond about his
adventure when he returned!

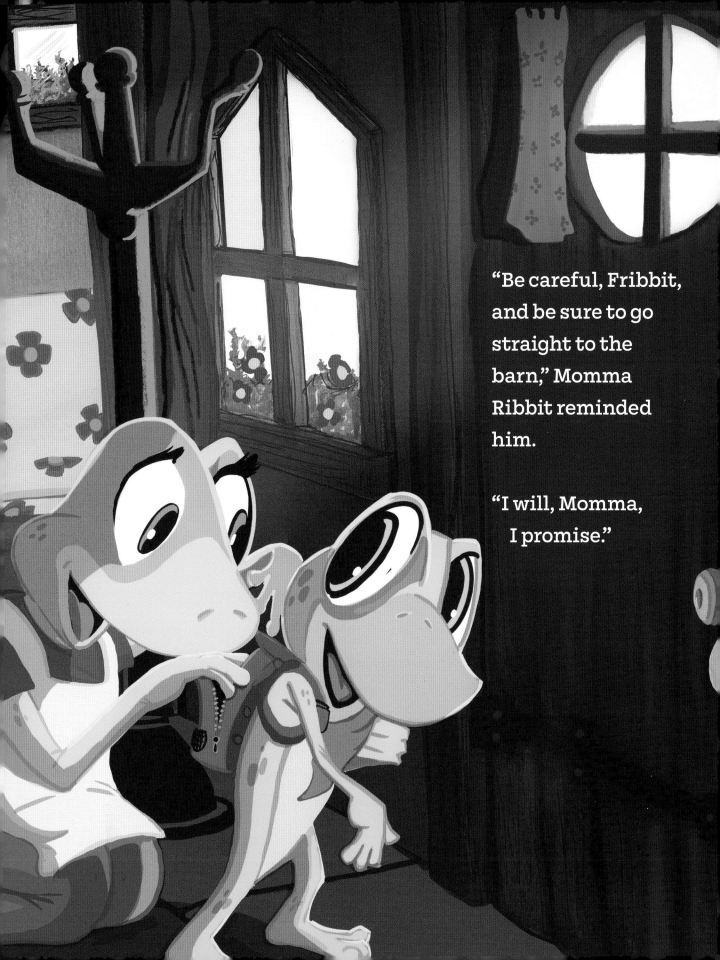

"Be careful, Fribbit, and be sure to go straight to the barn," Momma Ribbit reminded him.

"I will, Momma, I promise."

Fribbit started on his way. It wasn't long before he could no longer see Brightly Pond. He was a little nervous as the pond disappeared in the distance. He had never been this far on his own, but just then, his best friend Darby Dragonfly swooped down by his side.

"Good morning, Fribbit! Where are you headed?"

"I'm going to see Polly and Billy," Fribbit replied, eager to share his exciting news.

"All alone?" Darby said with surprise.

"Yes, Momma says I can go on my own today as long as I head straight to the barn," Fribbit said. "Why don't you come along with me? You can help me make sure I stay on the correct path, and we can play games with Billy and Polly."

"Oh, that sounds like so much fun!" Darby said.

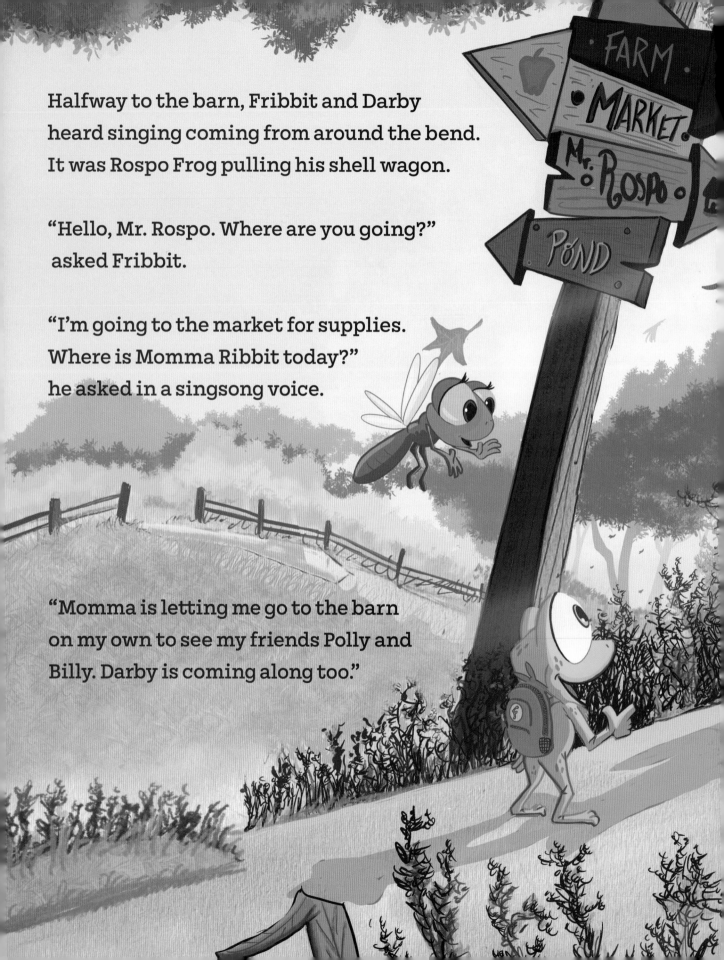

Halfway to the barn, Fribbit and Darby heard singing coming from around the bend. It was Rospo Frog pulling his shell wagon.

"Hello, Mr. Rospo. Where are you going?" asked Fribbit.

"I'm going to the market for supplies. Where is Momma Ribbit today?" he asked in a singsong voice.

"Momma is letting me go to the barn on my own to see my friends Polly and Billy. Darby is coming along too."

FARM

MARKET

Mr. Rospo

POND

"Going to the other end of the farm on your own is a big step for you, Fribbit. You're growing up," said Mr. Rospo. "You two stop by on your way back, and I'll give you some food from the market to bring to your mother."

Mr. Rospo continued singing his song as he headed down another path with his sparkly shell wagon. Fribbit and Darby continued on their way too.

As the opening in the trees to the farm pasture got closer, Fribbit became excited. It would be a fun surprise for his friends to learn that he made the trip without his mother.

While on the path, the pair was startled by a noise they heard in the bushes off the trail.

"What is that sound?" asked Fribbit nervously.

"I think we're being followed. I'll fly over and see who it is," said Darby. She was the less nervous of the two—not much scared her. That is what made them a great team.

Darby flew high above to get a better view. She saw something peeking through the bushes and flew down to take a closer look.

"It's Ruby Rabbit!" shouted Darby. Ruby is a friend who lives in the tree beside Brightly Pond.

"Hi, Ruby. What are you doing here?" asked Darby.

"I'm gathering food. Where are you two going?" she replied.

"We're headed to the barn to see
Polly and Billy. Want to join us?" asked Fribbit.

"I'd love to! I can collect apples that have fallen from
the tree in the pasture."

So Fribbit, Darby, and Ruby continued down the path.

"There they are!" shouted Darby.
They saw Billy Bull and Polly Pig sitting
in the field under the big apple tree.

In his low voice, Billy asked Polly,
"Is that Fribbit coming this way?"

"Yes, it's Fribbit!" Polly happily shouted.
"He's with Darby and Ruby too!"

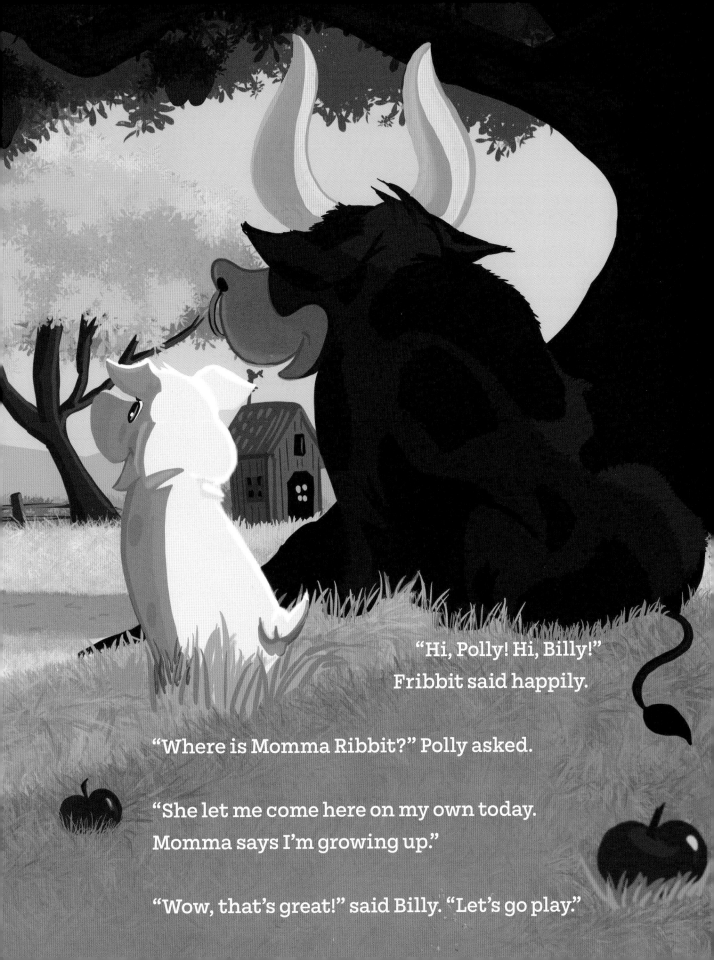

"Hi, Polly! Hi, Billy!"
Fribbit said happily.

"Where is Momma Ribbit?" Polly asked.

"She let me come here on my own today.
Momma says I'm growing up."

"Wow, that's great!" said Billy. "Let's go play."

They played under the apple tree
for hours until the sun began to set.
Now it was time to head back home to
Brightly Pond.

They said goodbye, and the trio headed
down the path toward home.

Back at the pond, Momma was sitting on a rock waiting anxiously for Fribbit to return home. Suddenly, she heard laughing and singing in the distance. It was Fribbit, Darby, Ruby, and Mr. Rospo coming up the path.

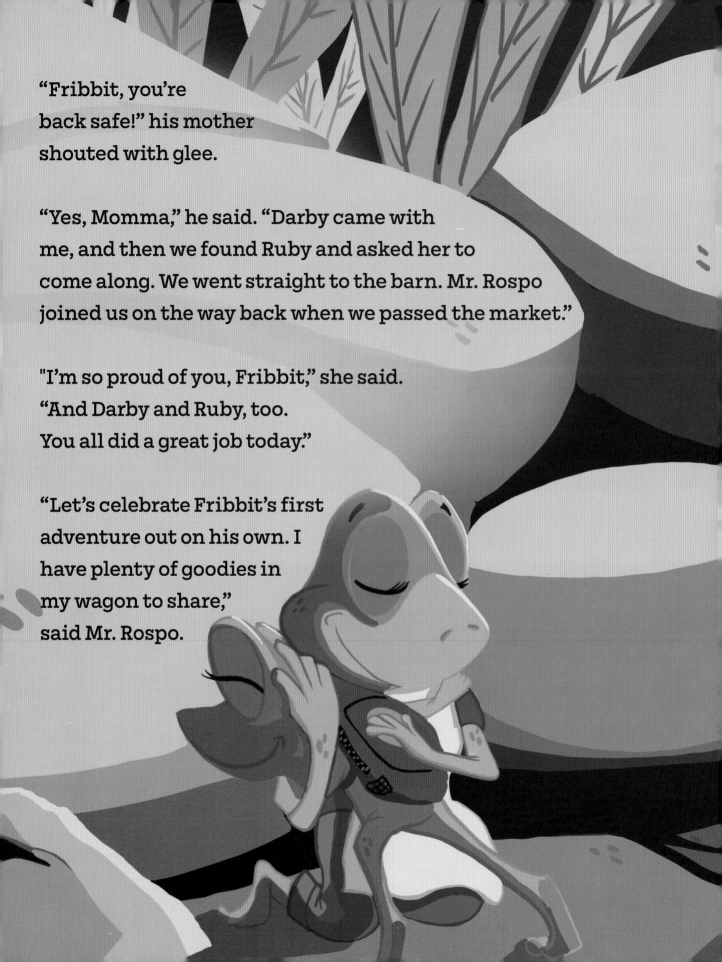

"Fribbit, you're
back safe!" his mother
shouted with glee.

"Yes, Momma," he said. "Darby came with
me, and then we found Ruby and asked her to
come along. We went straight to the barn. Mr. Rospo
joined us on the way back when we passed the market."

"I'm so proud of you, Fribbit," she said.
"And Darby and Ruby, too.
You all did a great job today."

"Let's celebrate Fribbit's first
adventure out on his own. I
have plenty of goodies in
my wagon to share,"
said Mr. Rospo.

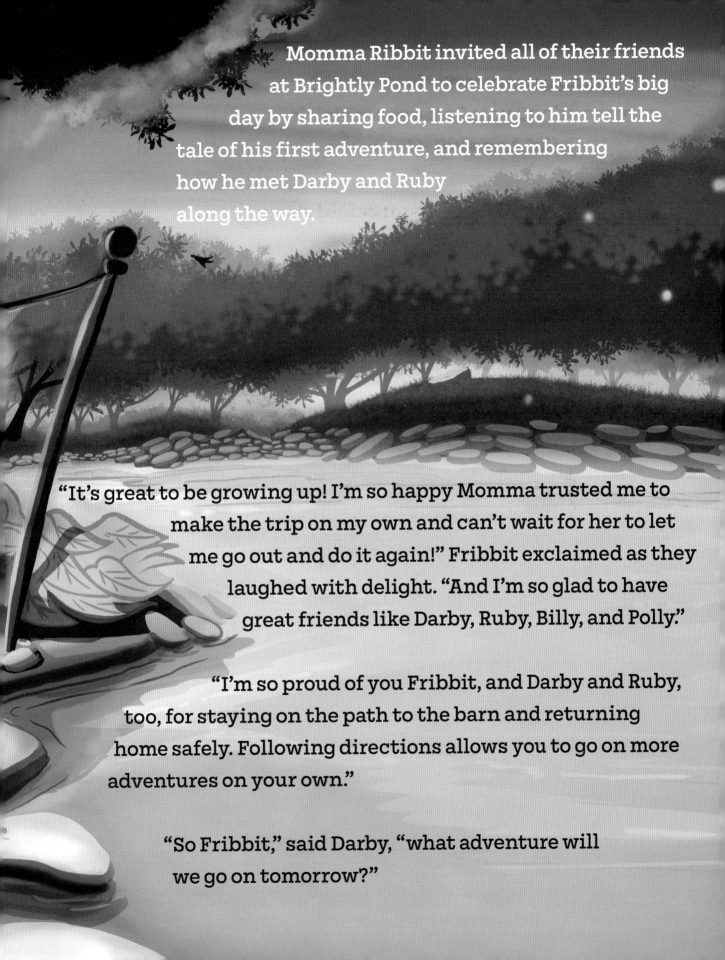

Momma Ribbit invited all of their friends at Brightly Pond to celebrate Fribbit's big day by sharing food, listening to him tell the tale of his first adventure, and remembering how he met Darby and Ruby along the way.

"It's great to be growing up! I'm so happy Momma trusted me to make the trip on my own and can't wait for her to let me go out and do it again!" Fribbit exclaimed as they laughed with delight. "And I'm so glad to have great friends like Darby, Ruby, Billy, and Polly."

"I'm so proud of you Fribbit, and Darby and Ruby, too, for staying on the path to the barn and returning home safely. Following directions allows you to go on more adventures on your own."

"So Fribbit," said Darby, "what adventure will we go on tomorrow?"

About the Authors

Gary Intili

Gary Intili was inspired to write *Brightly Pond* after the announcement that he was going to be a Poppy for his first grandchild. Over the years, Gary has collected small figurines of pond, woodland, and farm animals while at antique and craft sales, and one day created names and stories in his head for these statuettes to tell his future grandchild. Thus, Fribbit's world was created!

Gary lives in Dacula, Georgia, with his wife of thirty-one years, and is a woodworker, an athlete, and a fisherman. Gary is the father of two wonderful children and Poppy to his beautiful granddaughter.

Leighann Troino

After the birth of her daughter, Leighann Troino teamed up with her father, Gary, to cowrite *Brightly Pond* to bring to life the animals of Fribbit's world. Leighann grew up in Dacula, Georgia, after moving from New York as a child. Over the years, Leighann has delved into sign making, calligraphy, knitting, and now writing. She has a degree in developmental psychology and was previously an elementary and middle school teacher before diving into telecommunications. Leighann still lives in Georgia with her husband, Anthony, and their daughter, Elliana.